In Like
a Lion
Out Like
a Lamb

In Like a Lion
Out Like a Lamb

by **Marion Dane Bauer**

illustrated by **Emily Arnold McCully**

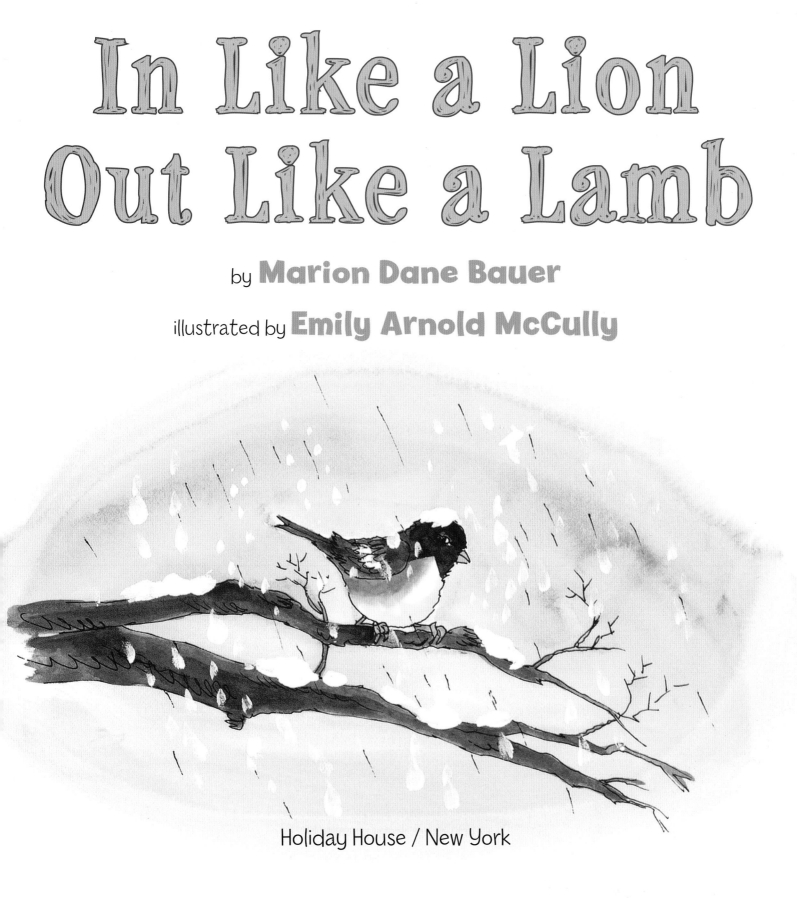

Holiday House / New York

March comes with a roar.
He rattles your windows
and scratches at your door.

He turns snow to mud,
then tromps across your floor.

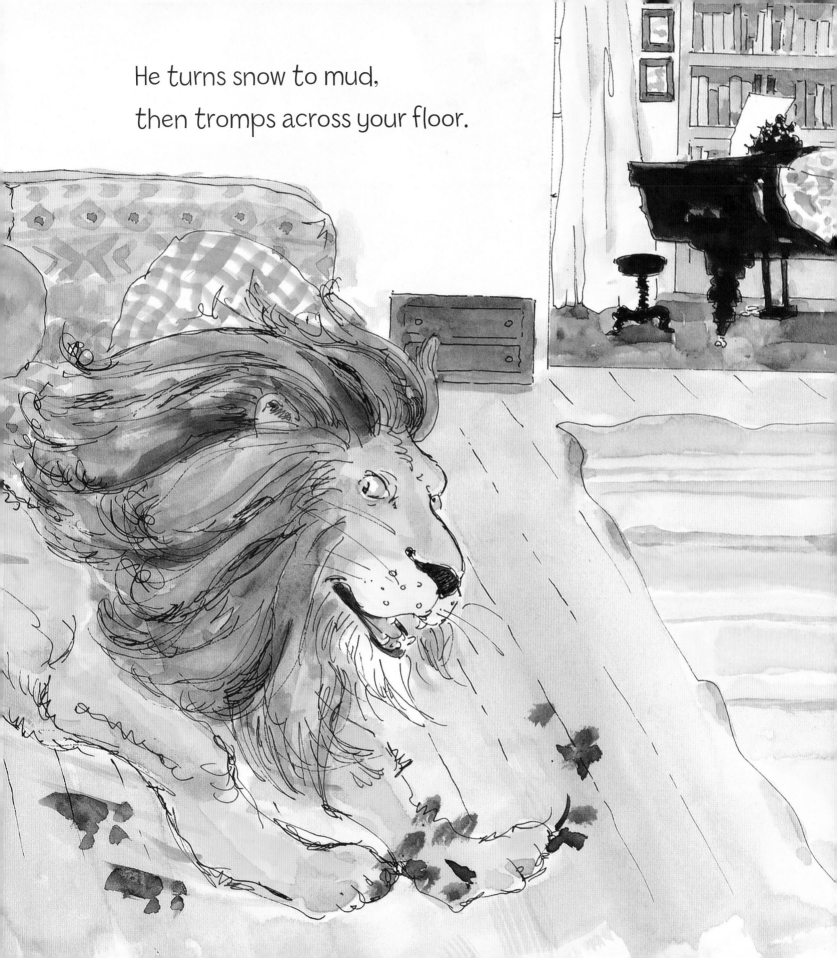

March comes with winter clinging to his tail.
He scatters sleet
and sometimes even hail.

"Were you expecting spring?" he snickers.

"Reach for your slickers."

March comes with a pounce and a growl.

Just step outside and hear him howl.

If you howl back,
will he go away?
Not very likely!
This lion means to stay
and stay
and stay.

Then one soft morning
wind gives way to breeze.
Buds pop out on trees.
The air is full of chickadees
and bumblebees.

And the lion takes a whiff, a sniff,
and lets out an enormous sneeze.

And guess who
comes riding in,
gliding in,
striding in
on that A-A-A-A-CHOO!

So . . .

where will the March lion go?
Will he wander to and fro,
defeated and lost,
predicting frost?

Or will he skulk through the greening grass,
eyes scheming,
teeth gleaming,
waiting for the lamb to pass?

No, never!

This fellow is much too clever.

He finds himself a sunny spot.

He stretches, yawns,

and curls into a knot.

And that rumbling noise you hear?
Never fear.
This lion is done with roaring,
and now he's snoring!
At least until next year.

Today the lamb's in charge
of grass and flowers,
sunshine and showers;
of babies,
small and large.

Come, all you babies.
Just hear March sing.
"Ba-a-a-a!" she says.
"Ba-a-a-a!" and "Ba-a-a-a!" again.

"It's spring!"

A-A-A-A-CHOO!

For everyone who loves weather,
as I do,
lion or lamb
— M. D. B.

For Ethan Quinn McCully
— E. A. M.

Text copyright © 2011 by Marion Dane Bauer
Illustrations copyright © 2011 by Emily Arnold McCully
All Rights Reserved
HOLIDAY HOUSE is registered in the U.S. Patent and Trademark Office.
Printed and bound in October 2020 at Tien Wah Press, Johor Bahru, Johor, Malaysia.
The text typeface is Billy Light.
The artwork was created with pen and ink and watercolor.
www.holidayhouse.com
7 9 10 8

Library of Congress Cataloging-in-Publication Data
Bauer, Marion Dane.
In like a lion, out like a lamb / by Marion Dane Bauer ; illustrated by Emily Arnold McCully. — 1st ed.
p. cm.
Summary: Describes in verse the lion that is March weather,
which finally gives way to the lamb of spring.
ISBN 978-0-8234-2238-8 (hardcover)
[1. Stories in rhyme. 2. March (Month)—Fiction. 3. Spring—Fiction.]
I. McCully, Emily Arnold, ill. II. Title.
PZ8.3.B3199In 2012
[E]—dc22
2010007892
ISBN 978-0-8234-2432-0 (paperback)